# Mayor Bunny's Chocolate Town

## Elys Dolan

OXFORD
UNIVERSITY PRESS

For all the Debbies out there, trying to tell the truth.

**OXFORD**
UNIVERSITY PRESS

Great Clarendon Street, Oxford OX2 6DP
Oxford University Press is a department of the University of Oxford.
It furthers the University's objective of excellence in research, scholarship,
and education by publishing worldwide. Oxford is a registered trade mark of
Oxford University Press in the UK and in certain other countries

Text and illustrations copyright © Elys Dolan 2022

The moral rights of the author and illustrator have been asserted
Database right Oxford University Press (maker)

First published 2022

British Library Cataloguing in Publication Data

Data available

ISBN: 978-0-19-278270-0 (hardback)
ISBN: 978-0-19-274623-8 (paperback)

10 9 8 7 6 5 4 3 2 1

Printed in China

Paper used in the production of this book is a natural, recyclable
product made from wood grown in sustainable forests.
The manufacturing process conforms to the environmental
regulations of the country of origin.

# CAN YOU EVER HAVE TOO MUCH CHOCOLATE?

Mr Bunny didn't think so. He used to run a whole chocolate factory. Then something happened that made him change his management style. Now he works as a team with the chickens and a quality-control unicorn called Edgar.

But Mr Bunny missed being in charge. No one took any notice of him or did what he said. It just wasn't the same.

Mr Bunny overheard the gossip and knew this was his chance.

Mr Bunny's team knew it wouldn't be easy.

It was time for Mr Bunny and Debbie to make their speeches and tell everyone why they would be the best mayor.

Debbie and her team had a plan.
They put up some posters to put an end to Mr Bunny's lies.

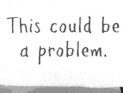

Debbie didn't think this was the right way for a candidate to behave.

At last it was time for the chickens to decide who would be their mayor, but even on election day Debbie could see that Mr Bunny was up to something.

Team Debbie were sure that the chickens would know better than to vote for a cheater.

The chickens couldn't wait to see how their new mayor would fix the town with chocolate. Everyone was delighted . . .

Once he was bored of his party, Mayor Bunny ordered lots and lots of chocolate to be sent from the factory to the town.

But when it got there the chickens didn't know what to do with it.

The chickens took cover in the factory.

But they weren't worried, they had a mayor to sort things out.

The chickens pushed Mayor Bunny out of the factory door to go and deal with the wasps.

Luckily, help was on the way.

With Mayor Debbie in charge
things were looking up.

But what became of Mr Bunny?

Debbie created a new job, just for him.

He's not in charge but Mr Bunny is OK with that.
Being the leader wasn't all it was cracked up to be.